GOLDILOCKS AND THE THREE BEARS
> This famous wicked little tale
> Should never have been put on sale.
> It is a mystery to me
> Why loving parents cannot see
> That this is actually a book
> About a brazen little crook. . . .

ROALD DAHL'S REVOLTING RHYMES
"You won't get through these airy fairy-tale revisions with a straight face. . . . How could the giant 'smell' an Englishman? Simple. Jack never took a bath." —*Kirkus Reviews*

"In bouncy verse and pithy language, Dahl gives his own irreverent versions of some familiar fairy tales, and Blake's scrabbly, lively line-and-wash pictures capture the mood of manic lampoon." —*Bulletin of the Center for Children's Books*

ROALD DAHL'S
REVOLTING
RHYMES

Illustrations by
QUENTIN BLAKE

A BANTAM SKYLARK BOOK®
TORONTO · NEW YORK · LONDON · SYDNEY · AUCKLAND

This low-priced Bantam Book
has been completely reset in a typeface
designed for easy reading, and was printed
from new plates. It contains the complete
text of the original hard-cover edition.
NOT ONE WORD HAS BEEN OMITTED.

RL 5, 008–011

ROALD DAHL'S REVOLTING RHYMES
A Bantam Book / published by arrangement with
Alfred A. Knopf, Inc.

PRINTING HISTORY
Originally published in Great Britain by Jonathan Cape Ltd., London
Alfred A. Knopf edition published March 1983
Bantam Skylark edition / April 1986

ISBN 0-553-15361-7

Published simultaneously in the United States and Canada

PRINTED IN THE UNITED STATES OF AMERICA

CW   0 9 8 7 6 5 4 3 2 1

ROALD DAHL'S
REVOLTING
RHYMES

Cinderella

I guess you think you know this story.
You don't. The real one's much more gory.
The phoney one, the one you know,
Was cooked up years and years ago,
And made to sound all soft and sappy
Just to keep the children happy.
Mind you, they got the first bit right,
The bit where, in the dead of night,

The Ugly Sisters, jewels and all,
Departed for the Palace Ball,
While darling little Cinderella
Was locked up in the slimy cellar,
Where rats who wanted things to eat
Began to nibble at her feet.
She bellowed, "Help!" and "Let me out!"
The Magic Fairy heard her shout.
Appearing in a blaze of light,
She said, "My dear, are you all right?"
"*All right?*" cried Cindy. "Can't you see
I feel as rotten as can be!"
She beat her fist against the wall,
And shouted, "Get me to the Ball!
There is a Disco at the Palace!
The rest have gone and I am jalous!
I want a dress! I want a coach!
And earrings and a diamond brooch!
And silver slippers, two of those!
And lovely nylon pantyhose!
Thereafter it will be a cinch
To hook the handsome Royal Prince!"
The Fairy said, "Hang on a tick."
She gave her Wand a mighty flick
And quickly, in no time at all,
Cindy was at the Palace Ball!

It made the Ugly Sisters wince
To see her dancing with the Prince.
She held him very tight and pressed
Herself against his manly chest.
The Prince himself was turned to pulp,
All *he* could do was gasp and gulp.
Then midnight struck. She shouted "Heck!
I've got to run to save my neck!"
The Prince cried, "No! Alas! Alack!"
He grabbed her dress to hold her back.
As Cindy shouted, "Let me go!"
The dress was ripped from head to toe.
She ran out in her underwear,
But lost one slipper on the stair.
The Prince was on it like a dart,

He pressed it to his pounding heart,
"The girl this slipper fits," he cried,
"Tomorrow morn shall be my bride!
I'll visit every house in town
Until I've tracked the maiden down!"
Then rather carelessly, I fear,
He placed it on a crate of beer.

At once, one of the Ugly Sisters,
(The one whose face was blotched with blisters)
Sneaked up and grabbed the dainty shoe,
And quickly flushed it down the loo.
Then in its place she calmly put
The slipper from her own left foot.
Ah-ha, you see, the plot grows thicker,
And Cindy's luck starts looking sicker.
Next day, the Prince went charging down
To knock on all the doors in town.
In every house, the tension grew.
Who was the owner of the shoe?
The shoe was huge and frightfully wide.
(A normal foot got lost inside.)

Also it smelled a wee bit icky.
(The owner's feet were hot and sticky.)
Thousands of eager people came
To try it on, but all in vain.
Now came the Ugly Sisters' go.
One tried it on. The Prince screamed "No!"
But she screamed, "Yes! It fits! Whoopee!
So now you've got to marry me!"

The Prince went white from ear to ear.
He muttered, "Let's get out of here."
"Oh no you don't! You've made a vow!
There's no way you can back out now!"
"Off with her head!" the Prince roared back.
They chopped it off with one big whack.
This pleased the Prince. He smiled and said,
"She's prettier without her head."
Then up came Sister Number Two,
Who yelled, "Now *I* will try the shoe!"

"Try this instead!" the Prince yelled back.
He swung his trusty sword and *smack*—
Her head went crashing to the ground.
It bounced a bit and rolled around.
In the kitchen, peeling spuds,
Cinderella heard the thuds
Of bouncing heads upon the floor,
And poked her own head round the door.
"What's all the racket?" Cindy cried.
"Mind your own bizz," the Prince replied.
Poor Cindy's heart was torn to shreds.
My Prince! she thought. He chops off *heads*!
How could I marry anyone
Who does that sort of thing for fun?
The Prince cried, "Who's this dirty slut?
Off with her nut! Off with her nut!"
Just then, all in a blaze of light,
The Magic Fairy hove in sight,
Her Magic Wand went *swoosh* and *swish*!
"Cindy!" she cried, "Come make a wish!
Wish anything and have no doubt
That I will make it come about!"
Cindy answered, "Oh kind Fairy,
This time I shall be more wary.
No more Princes, no more money.
I have had my taste of honey.
I'm wishing for a decent man.

They're hard to find. D'you think you can?"
Within a minute, Cinderella
Was married to a lovely feller,
A simple jam-maker by trade,
Who sold good homemade marmalade.
Their house was filled with smiles and laughter
And they were happy ever after.

Snow White
and the Seven Dwarfs

When little Snow White's mother died,
  The king, her father, up and cried,
"Oh, what a nuisance! What a life!
Now I must find another wife!"
(It's never easy for a king
To find himself that sort of thing.)
He wrote to every magazine
And said, "I'm looking for a Queen."
At least ten thousand girls replied
And begged to be the royal bride.
The king said with a shifty smile,
"I'd like to give each one a trial."
However, in the end he chose
A lady called Miss Maclahose,
Who brought along a curious toy
That seemed to give her endless joy—
This was a mirror framed in brass,
A MAGIC TALKING LOOKING GLASS.
Ask it something day or night,
It always got the answer right.

For instance, if you were to say,
"Oh Mirror, what's for lunch today?"
The thing would answer in a trice,
"Today it's scrambled eggs and rice."
Now every day, week in, week out,
The spoiled and stupid Queen would shout,
"Oh Mirror Mirror on the wall,
Who is the fairest of them all?"

The Mirror answered every time,
"Oh Madam, you're the Queen sublime.
You are the only one to charm us,
Queen, you are the cat's pajamas."
For ten whole years the silly Queen
Repeated this absurd routine.

Then suddenly, one awful day
She heard the Magic Mirror say,
"From now on, Queen, you're *Number Two*.
Snow White is prettier than you!"
The Queen went absolutely wild.
She yelled, "I'm going to scrag that child!
I'll cook her flaming goose! I'll skin 'er!
I'll have her rotten guts for dinner!"
She called the Huntsman to her study.
She shouted at him, "Listen buddy!
You drag that filthy girl outside,
And see you take her for a ride!
Thereafter slit her ribs apart
And bring me back her bleeding heart!"
The Huntsman dragged the lovely child
Deep deep into the forest wild.
Fearing the worst, poor Snow White spake.

She cried, "Oh please give me a break!"
The knife was poised, the arm was strong,
She cried again, "I've done no *wrong*!"
The Huntsman's heart began to flutter.
It melted like a pound of butter.
He murmured, "Okay, beat it, kid,"
And you can bet your life she did.
Later, the Huntsman made a stop
Within the local butcher's shop,
And there he bought, for safety's sake,
A bullock's heart and one nice steak.
"Oh Majesty! Oh Queen!" he cried,
"That rotten little girl has died!
And just to prove I didn't cheat,
I've brought along these bits of meat."
The Queen cried out, "Bravissimo!
I trust you killed her nice and slow."
Then (this is the disgusting part)
The Queen sat down and ate the heart!
(I only hope she cooked it well.
Boiled heart can be as tough as hell.)
While all of this was going on,
Oh where, oh where had Snow White gone?

She'd found it easy, being pretty,
To hitch a ride into the city,
And there she'd got a job, unpaid,
As general cook and parlor maid
With seven funny little men,
Each one not more than three foot ten,
Ex-horse-race jockeys, all of them.
These Seven Dwarfs, though awfully nice,
Were guilty of one shocking vice—
They squandered all of their resources
At the race track backing horses.
(When they hadn't backed a winner,
None of them got any dinner.)
One evening, Snow White said, "Look here,
I think I've got a great idea.
Just leave it all to me, okay?
And no more gambling till I say."
That very night, at eventide,
Young Snow White hitched another ride,
And then, when it was very late,
She slipped in through the Palace gate.
The King was in the counting house
Counting out the money,
The Queen was in the parlor
Eating bread and honey,
The footmen and the servants slept

16

So no one saw her as she crept
On tiptoe through the mighty hall
And grabbed THE MIRROR off the wall.
As soon as she had got it home,
She told the Senior Dwarf (or Gnome)
To ask it what he wished to know.
"Go on!" she shouted. "Have a go!"
He said, "Oh Mirror, please don't joke!
Each one of us is stony broke!
Which horse will win tomorrow's race,
The Ascot Gold Cup Steeplechase?"
The Mirror whispered sweet and low,
"The horse's name is Mistletoe."
The Dwarfs went absolutely daft,
They kissed young Snow White fore and aft,
Then rushed away to raise some dough
With which to back old Mistletoe.

They pawned their watches, sold the car,
They borrowed money near and far,
(For much of it they had to thank
The manager of Barclays Bank).
They went to Ascot and of course
For once they backed the winning horse.
Thereafter, every single day,
The Mirror made the bookies pay.
Each Dwarf and Snow White got a share,
And each was soon a millionaire,
Which shows that gambling's not a sin
Provided that you always win.

Jack and the Beanstalk

Jack's mother said, "We're *stony broke!*
Go out and find some wealthy bloke
Who'll buy our cow. Just say she's sound
And worth at least a hundred pound.
But don't you dare to let him know
That she's as old as billy-o."
Jack led the old brown cow away,
And came back later in the day,
And said, "Oh Mumsie dear, guess what
Your clever little boy has got.
I got, I really don't know how,
A super trade-in for our cow."
The mother said, "You little creep,
I'll bet you sold her much too cheap."
When Jack produced one lousy bean,
His startled mother, turning green,
Leaped high up in the air and cried,
"I'm *absolutely stupefied!*
You crazy boy! D'you really mean
You sold our Daisy for a bean?"
She snatched the bean. She yelled, "You chump!"
And flung it on the rubbish dump.

Then summoning up all her power,
She beat the boy for half an hour,
Using (and nothing could be meaner)
The handle of a vacuum cleaner.
At ten p.m. or thereabout,
The little bean began to sprout.
By morning it had grown so tall
You couldn't see the top at all.
Young Jack cried, "Mum, admit it now!
It's better than a rotten cow!"
The mother said, "You lunatic!
Where are the beans that I can pick?
There's not *one bean*! It's bare as bare!"
"No no!" cried Jack. "You look up there!
Look very high and you'll behold
Each single leaf is solid gold!"

By gollikins, the boy was right!
Now, glistening in the morning light,
The mother actually perceives
A mass of lovely golden leaves!
She yells out loud, "My sainted souls!
I'll sell the Mini, buy a Rolls!
Don't stand and gape, you little clot!
Get up there quick and grab the lot!"
Jack was nimble, Jack was keen.
He scrambled up the mighty bean.
Up up he went without a stop,

24

But just as he was near the top,
A ghastly frightening thing occurred—
Not far above his head he heard
A big deep voice, a rumbling thing
That made the very heavens ring.
It shouted loud, "FEE FI FO FUM
I SMELL THE BLOOD OF AN ENGLISHMAN!"

Jack was frightened, Jack was quick,
And down he climbed in half a tick.
"Oh Mum!" he gasped. "Believe you me
There's something nasty up our tree!
I saw him, Mum! My gizzard froze!
A Giant with a clever nose!"
"A *clever nose!*" his mother hissed.
"You must be going round the twist!"
"He smelled me out, I swear it, Mum!
He said he *smelled* an Englishman!"

The mother said, "And well he might!
I've told you every single night
To take a bath because you reek!
But would you listen to me speak?
You even make your mother shrink
Because of your unholy stink!"

Jack answered, "Well, if you're so clean
Why don't *you* climb the crazy bean."
The mother cried, "By gad, I will!
There's life within the old dog still!"
She hitched her skirts above her knee
And disappeared right up the tree.

Now would the Giant smell his mum?
Jack listened for the *fee-fo-fum*.
He gazed aloft. He wondered when
The dreaded words would come . . . And then .
From somewhere high above the ground
There came a frightful crunching sound.
He heard the Giant mutter twice,
"By gosh, that tasted very nice.
Although," (and this in grumpy tones),
"I wish there weren't so many bones."
"By Christopher!" Jack cried. "By gum!
The Giant's eaten up my mum!
He smelled her out! She's in his belly!
I had a hunch that she was smelly."
Jack stood there gazing longingly
Upon the huge and golden tree.
He murmured softly, "Golly-gosh,
I guess I'll *have* to take a wash
If I am going to climb this tree
Without the Giant smelling me.
In fact, a bath's my only hope . . ."
He rushed indoors and grabbed the soap.
He scrubbed his body everywhere.
He even washed and rinsed his hair.
He did his teeth, he blew his nose
And went out smelling like a rose.

Once more he climbed the mighty bean.
The Giant sat there, gross, obscene,
Muttering through his vicious teeth
(While Jack sat tensely just beneath),
Muttering loud, "FEE FI FO FUM,
RIGHT NOW I CAN'T SMELL ANYONE."

Jack waited till the Giant slept,
Then out along the boughs he crept
And gathered so much gold, I swear
He was an instant millionaire.
"A bath," he said, "does seem to pay.
I'm going to have one every day."

Goldilocks and the
Three Bears

This famous wicked little tale
Should never have been put on sale.
It is a mystery to me
Why loving parents cannot see
That this is actually a book
About a brazen little crook.
Had I the chance I wouldn't fail
To clap young Goldilocks in jail.
Now just imagine how *you'd* feel
If you had cooked a lovely meal,
Delicious porridge, steaming hot,
Fresh coffee in the coffeepot,
With maybe toast and marmalade,
The table beautifully laid,
One place for you and one for Dad,
Another for your little lad.
Then Dad cries, "Golly-gosh! Gee-whiz!
Oh cripes! How hot this porridge is!
Let's take a walk along the street
Until it's cool enough to eat."

He adds, "An early morning stroll
Is good for people on the whole.
It makes your appetite improve,
It also helps your bowels to move."
No proper wife would dare to question
Such a sensible suggestion,
Above all not at breakfast time
When men are seldom in their prime.
No sooner are you down the road
Than Goldilocks, that little toad,
That nosey thieving little louse
Comes sneaking in your empty house.
She looks around. She quickly notes
Three bowls brimful of porridge-oats.
And while still standing on her feet,
She grabs a spoon and starts to eat.
I say again, how *would* you feel
If you had made this lovely meal

And some delinquent little tot
Broke in and gobbled up the lot?

But wait! That's not the worst of it!
Now comes the most distressing bit.
You are of course a house-proud wife,
And all your happy married life
You have collected lovely things
Like gilded cherubs wearing wings,
And furniture by Chippendale
Bought at some famous auction sale.
But your most special valued treasure,
The piece that gives you endless pleasure,
Is one small children's dining chair,
Elizabethan, very rare.
It is in fact your joy and pride,
Passed down to you on Grandma's side.
But Goldilocks, like many freaks,
Does not appreciate antiques.

She doesn't care, she doesn't mind,
And now she plonks her fat behind
Upon this dainty precious chair,
And crunch! It busts beyond repair.
A nice girl would at once exclaim,
"Oh dear! Oh heavens! What a shame!"
Not Goldie. She begins to swear.
She bellows, "What a lousy chair!"
And uses *one* disgusting word
That luckily you've never heard.
(I dare not write it, even hint it.
Nobody would ever print it.)
You'd think by now this little skunk
Would have the sense to do a bunk.
But no. I very much regret
She hasn't nearly finished yet.
Deciding she would like a rest,
She says, "Let's see which bed is best."
Upstairs she goes and tries all three.
(Here comes the next catastrophe.)
Most educated people choose
To rid themselves of socks and shoes
Before they clamber into bed.
But Goldie didn't give a shred.
Her filthy shoes were thick with grime,
And mud and mush and slush and slime.
Worse still, upon the heel of one

Was something that a dog had done.
I say once more, what *would* you think
If all this horrid dirt and stink
Was smeared upon your eiderdown
By this revolting little clown.
(The famous story has no clues
To show the girl removed her shoes.)
Oh, what a tale of crime on crime!
Let's check it for a second time.
Crime One, the prosecution's case:
She breaks and enters someone's place.

Crime Two, the prosecutor notes:
She steals a bowl of porridge-oats.

Crime Three: She breaks a precious chair
Belonging to the Baby Bear.
Crime Four: She smears each spotless sheet
With filthy messes from her feet.
A judge would say without a blink,
"Ten years hard labor in the clink!"
But in the book, as you will see,
The little beast gets off scot-free,

While tiny children near and far
Shout "Goody-good! Hooray! Hurrah!"
"Poor darling Goldilocks!" they say,
"Thank goodness that she got away!"

Myself, I think I'd rather send
Young Goldie to a sticky end.
"Oh Daddy!" cried the Baby Bear,
"My porridge gone! It isn't fair!"
"Then go upstairs," the Big Bear said,
"Your porridge is upon the bed.
But as it's inside mademoiselle,
You'll have to eat *her* up as well."

Little Red Riding Hood
and the Wolf

As soon as Wolf began to feel
That he would like a decent meal,
He went and knocked on Grandma's door.
When Grandma opened it, she saw
The sharp white teeth, the horrid grin,
And Wolfie said, "May I come in?"
Poor Grandmamma was terrified,
"He's going to eat me up!" she cried.

And she was absolutely right.
He ate her up in one big bite.
But Grandmamma was small and tough,
And Wolfie wailed, "That's not enough!
I haven't yet begun to feel
That I have had a decent meal!"
He ran around the kitchen yelping,
"I've *got* to have a second helping!"
Then added with a frightful leer,
"I'm therefore going to wait right here
Till Little Miss Red Riding Hood
Comes home from walking in the wood."
He quickly put on Grandma's clothes,
(Of course he hadn't eaten those).
He dressed himself in coat and hat.
He put on shoes and after that
He even brushed and curled his hair,
Then sat himself in Grandma's chair.
In came the little girl in red.
She stopped. She stared. And then she said,

"What great big ears you have, Grandma."
"All the better to hear you with," the Wolf replied.
"What great big eyes you have, Grandma,"
said Little Red Riding Hood.
"All the better to see you with," the Wolf replied.

He sat there watching her and smiled.
He thought, I'm going to eat this child.
Compared with her old Grandmamma
She's going to taste like caviar.

Then Little Red Riding Hood said, *"But Grandma,
what a lovely great big furry coat you have on."*

"That's wrong!" cried Wolf. "Have you forgot
To tell me what BIG TEETH I've got?
Ah well, no matter what you say,
I'm going to eat you anyway."
The small girl smiles. One eyelid flickers.
She whips a pistol from her knickers.
She aims it at the creature's head
And *bang bang bang,* she shoots him dead.
A few weeks later, in the wood,
I came across Miss Riding Hood.
But what a change! No cloak of red,
No silly hood upon her head.
She said, "Hello, and do please note
My lovely furry wolfskin coat."

The Three Little Pigs

The animal I really dig
Above all others is the pig.
Pigs are noble. Pigs are clever,
Pigs are courteous. However,
Now and then, to break this rule,
One meets a pig who is a fool.
What, for example, would you say
If strolling through the woods one day,
Right there in front of you you saw
A pig who'd built his house of STRAW?

The Wolf who saw it licked his lips,
And said, "That pig has had his chips."

"Little pig, little pig, let me come in!"
"No, no, by the hairs on my chinny-chin-chin!"
"Then I'll huff and I'll puff and I'll blow your house in!"

The little pig began to pray,
But Wolfie blew his house away.
He shouted, "Bacon, pork and ham!
Oh, what a lucky Wolf I am!"
And though he ate the pig quite fast,
He carefully kept the tail till last.
Wolf wandered on, a trifle bloated.
Surprise, surprise, for soon he noted

Another little house for pigs,
And this one had been built of TWIGS!

"Little pig, little pig, let me come in!"
"No, no, by the hairs on my chinny-chin-chin!"
"Then I'll huff and I'll puff and I'll blow your house in!"

The Wolf said, "Okay, here we go!"
He then began to blow and blow.
The little pig began to squeal.
He cried, "Oh Wolf, you've had *one* meal!
Why can't we talk and make a deal?"
The Wolf replied, "Not on your nelly!"
And soon the pig was in his belly.
"Two juicy little pigs!" Wolf cried,
"But still I am not satisfied!
I know full well my tummy's bulging,
But oh, how I adore indulging."
So creeping quietly as a mouse,
The Wolf approached another house,
A house which also had inside
A little piggy trying to hide.
But this one, Piggy Number Three,
Was bright and brainy as could be.
No straw for him, no twigs or sticks.
This pig had built his house of BRICKS.
"You'll not get me!" the Piggy cried.

"I'll blow you down!" the Wolf replied.
"You'll need," Pig said, "a lot of puff,
And I don't think you've got enough."
Wolf huffed and puffed and blew and blew.
The house stayed up as good as new.
"If I can't blow it *down*," Wolf said,
"I'll have to blow it *up* instead.
I'll come back in the dead of night
And blow it up with dynamite!"
Pig cried, "You brute! I might have known!"
Then, picking up the telephone,
He dialed as quickly as he could
The number of Red Riding Hood.
"Hello," she said. "Who's speaking? *Who?*

51

Oh, hello Piggy, how d'you do?"
Pig cried, "I need your help, Miss Hood!
Oh help me, please! D'you think you could?"
"I'll try, of course," Miss Hood replied.
"What's on your mind . . . ?" "A *Wolf!*" Pig cried.
"I know you've dealt with wolves before,
And now I've got one at my door!"
"My darling Pig," she said, "my sweet,
That's something *really* up my street.
I've just begun to wash my hair.
But when it's dry, I'll be right there."
A short while later, through the wood,
Came striding brave Miss Riding Hood.
The Wolf stood there, his eyes ablaze
And yellowish, like mayonnaise.
His teeth were sharp, his gums were raw,
And spit was dripping from his jaw.
Once more the maiden's eyelid flickers.
She draws the pistol from her knickers.
Once more, she hits the vital spot,
And kills him with a single shot.
Pig, peeping through the window, stood
And yelled, "Well done, Miss Riding Hood!"

Ah, Piglet, you must never trust
Young ladies from the upper crust.

For now, Miss Riding Hood, one notes,
Not only has *two* wolfskin coats,
But when she goes from place to place,
She has a PIGSKIN TRAVELING CASE.

ABOUT THE AUTHOR

ROALD DAHL is the author of some of the most widely read children's books ever published, including *Charlie and the Chocolate Factory, James and the Giant Peach, Danny the Champion of the World, The Wonderful Story of Henry Sugar, The Twits, George's Marvelous Medicine,* and *The Enormous Crocodile.* He is also celebrated for his wonderfully wicked short stories for adults. Mr. Dahl was born in Wales and now lives in Buckinghamshire, England.

ABOUT THE ILLUSTRATOR

QUENTIN BLAKE has illustrated many favorite children's books, among them *The Enormous Crocodile, The Twits,* and *George's Marvelous Medicine* by Roald Dahl. He has also illustrated several of his own stories, most recently *Mister Magnolia,* which won the Kate Greenaway Medal. He is a frequent contributor to *Cricket* magazine, and since 1978 he has been Head of the Illustration Department in the School of Graphic Arts at the Royal College of Art in London.

ROALD DAHL

Roald Dahl's stories are funny and are filled with unexpected twists, so they are favorites with kids who love reading zany and unlikely tales.

Buy them at your local bookstore or use this handy coupon for ordering:

Bantam Books, Inc., Dept. RD1, 414 East Golf Road, Des Plaines, Ill. 60016

Please send me the books I have checked above. I am enclosing $_____ (please add $1.50 to cover postage and handling. Send check or money order—no cash or C.O.D.'s please).

Mr/Ms/Miss _____

Address _____

City _____ State/Zip _____

RD1—1/86

Please allow four to six weeks for delivery. This offer expires 7/86.

Bantam Skylark Paperbacks
The Kid-Pleasers

Especially designed for easy reading with large type, wide margins and captivating illustrations, Skylarks are "kid-pleasing" paperbacks featuring the authors, subjects and characters children love.

☐	15258	BANANA BLITZ Florence Parry Heide	$2.25
☐	15259	FREAKY FILLINS #1 David Hartley	$1.95
☐	15250	THE GOOD-GUY CAKE Barbara Dillion	$1.95
☐	15381	C.L.U.T.Z. Marilyn Wilkes	$2.25
☐	15384	MUSTARD Charlotte Graeber	$2.25
☐	15157	ALVIN FERNALD: TV ANCHORMAN Clifford Hicks	$1.95
☐	15338	ANASTASIA KRUPNIK Lois Lowry	$2.50
☐	15168	HUGH PINE Janwillem Van de Wetering	$1.95
☐	15248	CHARLIE AND THE CHOCOLATE FACTORY Roald Dahl	$2.50
☐	15174	CHARLIE AND THE GREAT GLASS ELEVATOR Roald Dahl	$2.50
☐	15317	JAMES AND THE GIANT PEACH Roald Dahl	$2.95
☐	15255	ABEL'S ISLAND William Steig	$2.25
☐	15194	BIG RED Jim Kjelgaard	$2.50
☐	15206	IRISH RED: SON OF BIG RED Jim Kjelgaard	$2.25
☐	42075	JACOB TWO-TWO MEETS THE HOODED FANG Mordecai Richler	$2.95
☐	15343	THE TWITS Roald Dahl	$2.50

Prices and availability subject to change without notice.

Buy them at your local bookstore or use this handy coupon for ordering:

Shop at home
for quality childrens books
and save money, too.

Now you can order books for the whole family from Bantam's latest listing of hundreds of titles including many fine children's books. *And* this special offer gives you an opportunity to purchase a Bantam book for only 50¢. Here's how:

By ordering any five books at the regular price per order, you can also choose any other single book listed (up to $4.95 value) for just 50¢. Some restrictions do apply, so for further details send for Bantam's listing of titles today.